Warren McCain

A Soldier's Diary

The History of Company L, Third Indiana Cavalry

Warren McCain

A Soldier's Diary
The History of Company L, Third Indiana Cavalry

ISBN/EAN: 9783337120542

Printed in Europe, USA, Canada, Australia, Japan

Cover: Foto ©Raphael Reischuk / pixelio.de

More available books at **www.hansebooks.com**

——OR,——

THE HISTORY OF COMPANY "L,"

THIRD INDIANA CAVALRY.

——BY——

GENERAL WARREN McCAIN,
Late Sergeant of the Company.

——————·——————

INDIANAPOLIS:
WILLIAM A. PATTON, PUBLISHER.
1885.

PREFACE.

Twenty years have passed, and almost all forgotten
When I began to tell my experience in that land of cotton.

Many elaborate histories of the great War of the Rebellion
have been written, giving a general description of the armies and
all their important movements during the various campaigns,
together with a detailed account of many of the great Generals
and important officers. But this little book is designed only to
give an account of an individual company of the Third Indiana
Cavalry in the great Army of the Cumberland during a period of
nearly three years.

From a diary kept by myself during that eventful period I
have gleaned all the dates and little incidents which make up the
contents of this little book.

Several of my old comrades have urged me to give this account of our company during those perilous times, and I have
done it as much for their satisfaction as for my own interest and
pleasure. I know the boys will be glad to get this little scrap of
history, though each member of the company might be able to
add other valuable paragraphs to the same.

But however much to prevent it they may try,
If they will read it, they will both laugh, and cry.

G. W. McCain.

CONTENTS.

A SOLDIER'S DIARY;

—OR,—

THE HISTORY

—OF—

COMPANY "L," THIRD INDIANA CAVALRY.

This company, together with Company "M," were sworn into the United States service on the 23d day of October, 1862. The Government had raised the quota of cavalry regiments from ten to twelve companies, and these two companies had been raised to fill that quota in the Third Indiana Cavalry, the other ten companies having been in the field for about one year. These two companies had been enlisted with the understanding that they were to serve only for the unexpired term of the regiment; but when sworn in, it was for three years, or during the war, as the Government would not receive soldiers for a shorter term of service. However, for our encouragement, we were told that the war could not last more than two years.

The officers of our company ("L") were Captain O. M. Powers and Lieutenants George J. Langsdale and S. J. Mitchell. Our first camp was "Jo Reynolds," including "Blake's Woods," in the northwestern part of the city of Indianapolis, Indiana. We had been encamped here more than a month before we entered the Government service. Soon after this we moved from Camp Jo Reynolds to Camp Carrington, where we remained nearly one

year. This was a beautiful camp, and we enjoyed soldier life pretty well here, notwithstanding the frequent reports of the gardeners, who came in with their petty complaints to our officers concerning the loss of onions, lettuce, etc. I was First Duty Sergeant at that time, and I well remember one occasion, when we were enjoying a sumptuous dinner on lettuce, the Captain came down to our quarters and spoiled the whole thing by kicking over the pan of prepared lettuce and ordering me to take the whole mess to the guard-house. This was a little unpleasant duty for me, and several of the boys managed to get away before we reached that obnoxious place of confinement. We had a bad lot of neighbors living around Camp Carrington, and they were always complaining to our officers about stolen chickens and other little things, to the great annoyance of all the boys. Indeed, from their conduct, one would think they expected to find perfection among soldiers. We also had a well established suttler in our camp here, and he stood in with the head officers, and was doing a staving business. But the boys thought he was accumulating too fast off their small wages, so one night his shanty fell, and great was the fall thereof. His goods were soon scattered to the four winds, and it was with difficulty that he found a vestige of the whole stock within the camp. Soldiers were not much for accumulating, but they were great for scattering.

During our first year's service, we remained in our own State, doing camp duty, and making various scouts and raids in different parts of the State. The Government sent twenty-five of us to Morgan county after deserters at one time. We captured six of them, and then had a battle with a company of forty of the disloyal citizens of that county. They fired only one shot, and we put them to flight, killing one man and taking six prisoners.

It was during this year that the Democrats had their great convention at Indianapolis, when it was said they were going to take the arsenal and liberate the Rebel prisoners, etc. This was that momentous time at which was fought "*the bloodless battle of Pogue's Run*," in which Shelby county suffered the loss of so

many revolvers. One woman gave up six, which she had se-
creted in her bosom. Revolvers were found in the "Run"
many days after this disgraceful affair.

We also participated in the Morgan raid, going into Kentucky,
through Indiana and into Ohio, where General Morgan was captured. A good number of Company "L" were present with
General Shackelford, and took an active part in this capture.
Many a sleepless night we spent while on this raid, which lasted
about three weeks. I was sent several times into Shelby and
Decatur counties with a squad of four men to arrest deserters and
recover Government property. We had some interesting times
with members of the Golden Circle and the Rebel sympathizers
of those counties. But we received much encouragement and
many a good dinner from the loyal citizens.

We finally left Camp Carrington and moved over to Camp
Morton, where we remained until we left the State and marched
to the field in September, 1863. We first went to Cincinnati,
and then across the Ohio river to Covington, in Kentucky, where
we were fully equipped for field service. Here we drew our
first little "dog-tents." We marched through Kentucky by the
way of Camp Nelson and Crab Orchard to Cumberland Gap,
Tennessee. Rested here a short time, and then marched on
through Taswell, across Clinch river, and over that rugged
Clinch mountain, and on to Greenville, Tennessee. We went
into camp at this place, and here we remained from the 12th of
October to the 6th of November, 1863. Our camp was a very
pleasant one, situated a little east of Greenville. While here our
company performed the various duties common to the cavalry
service, and was ever prompt and active.

Now we just began to realize that we were indeed in the field,
far away from our base of supplies, and thrown almost entirely
upon our own resources. But we soon learned how to take care
of ourselves.

If any of the boys got sick, (no difference what the disease,)
they only had to apply to Dr. Lieutenant Langsdale, who dosed
them with capsicum, and they invariably got well.

The disease called "foot evil" here made its first attack on our horses, but it was soon eradicated by the skill and prompt attention of Dr. Ed. Mitchell, who was our horse ferrier.

We fell back to Lick-creek bridge on the night of the 6th of November, where we stayed ten days, scouting and doing picket duty. On the 16th we retreated still further back to Bull's Gap. Rested one day, drew rations, and then marched back to Cumberland Gap with General Wilcox and his whole command. We halted the first night at the foot of Clinch mountain, where we overtook General Shackelford's command. The camp fires in the "Clinch valley" that night displayed a most magnificent scene. There was encamped in this valley more than a division of soldiers, and their camp fires seemed to illuminate the whole valley and south side of the mountain. We rested here one day, and then performed that dreaded task of climbing Clinch mountain again. We reached Taswell on the 20th of the month, and stayed here one night. This was a deserted and desolate town. It had been a place of some considerable note before General Bragg's army passed through it, but now the principal buildings had been burned, and the entire town was but a pile of ruins.

On the 21st we re-entered Cumberland Gap, and pitched our tents three miles northeast of it, on the Virginia road. Here we began to realize something of the hardships of a soldier's life in the field. Had to live on beef and parched corn. The infantry had to live on this fare for several days, (two ears of corn being a day's ration,) but our cavalry boys took their corn to a mill and had it ground into meal, from which they made bread.

The "Gap" at this time had lost all its attractions for us. The Government supplies here were very limited, and we had to depend largely upon foraging for our subsistence. About the first of December we had the good luck to draw our back pay and some new clothing; but all this would not suffice for "grub," and the boys would often say that a new General had taken command of the "Gap," and when some one would ask, "Who?" the answer would be, "General Starvation." Our Captain, Quartermaster Sergeant and about thirty men of our company

were detailed to take a drove of convalescent horses back to
Camp Nelson, Ky. The remainder of the company was then
made a body guard for Colonel Curtin.

We again started southward, marching to Taswell the first day,
where we camped for the night. This was the first day of December, and this night will ever be remembered by us as one of
the saddest of that year on account of a dreadful accident that
occurred. Jahue Beech, a young man of our company, acci-
dentally shot and killed himself with his revolver. He was an
orphan boy, about 20 years of age. This was our first fatal accident, and I was the first one to behold the dying boy. It was a
most melancholy scene. Heavy cannonading was heard in the
direction of Walker's Ford, on the Clinch river, on the morning
of the 2d of December, and we left Taswell on a scouting expedition in that direction, watching for a flank movement of the
enemy.

The Twelfth Michigan Battery and several Indiana regiments
were now moving to the front. The fighting still continued, and
we were frequently near enough to hear the shells burst and the
report of the musketry, but a high ridge prevented us from seeing
the engagement. Our forces fell back a little and took a new
position about dark, when the firing ceased. The night was
dark and cold, and I rode alone seven miles back to Taswel or
rations for my hungry squad. I had long since been promoted
from First Duty Sergeant to Commissary Sergeant, and now to
see that the boys got their "grub" in due season was my chief
concern. We were out scouting on the 3d, but the enemy had
"skedaddled." I was very busy, but could not supply the demand for rations, consequently the boys were allowed to forage
again.

I took a small squad and went up into a mountain, where I
got corn enough to make five bushels of meal, and when we returned to camp, we found that other parties had been out and
had brought in a good supply of fresh pork. Marched back to
Taswell again on the 5th, and stayed here until the 7th, when
we once more started back on the old road to Clinch mountain.

Crossed the Clinch river about 4 p. m. Met a scouting party here that reported the "Rebs" in the vicinity of the mountain about 15,000 strong. We re-crossed the river, and went into camp about two miles west of it.

All the axes in the division were now collected together, and a large squad of men detailed to build pontoon bridges. We remained here several days while the bridges were being built.

Scouting parties were constantly going out and coming in, bringing dispatches concerning the Rebels, who were about four miles distant. There was considerable skirmishing done about this time.

The "Gorillas" got in between us and the mountain on the 13th and captured a train of twenty-five wagons, all loaded with our provisions. We gave chase but could not overtake them. We came upon their camp ground while their fires were yet brightly burning. They were not far in advance. It was a lucky thing for us that we did not overtake them, for we learned afterward that they had two brigades of cavalry. On learning this Colonel Curtin thinking it imprudent to venture further with his small detachment, retreated back to the Clinch river, which at this time was considerably swollen, making it necessary for us to cross in a boat towed by a rope and poles.

When we reached our camp at 4 a. m., our horses were jaded and we were all tired and sleepy. December 15th was a warm and very pleasant day, and we were on the southside of a mountain where the sun was shining brightly, causing everything to look cheerful and happy.

On the 16th we marched back to Sycamore Station. Cannonading was again heard in the direction of Walker's Ford, and our pickets were guarding the road leading in that direction. Rained all night the 17th. We moved up to Big Springs, where we staid until the 20th when we marched west to Walker's Ford. For several days we were kept marching back and forward here. We had crossed the river at this ford three times. Our marching to and fro here would remind one of playing a game of checkers,

Cumberland Gap and Knoxville representing the two king rows and the intervening country the main board.

From the first of the month when left the "Gap," up to this time, we had been very busy marching, scouting, foraging and running mills. In fact we had been acting the part of "Lackey boys" for the whole division. On Christmas day we were encamped on the battlefield where the engagement had taken place on the 2d of the month. We had marched from Big Springs, forded the Clinch River, climbed the stoney hills and got safely thus far. Christmas did not come to us, as usual, with all its merriments, but we were glad to see it come, for by its coming we were reminded that the time was fast passing away, and that our term of service was growing shorter. We were often at a loss to know the day of the week, and scarcely ever knew when Sunday came; but somehow we had found out that this was the great holiday of 1863, and we tried to enjoy it as best we could. We contrasted this Christmas with that of 1862, when we celebrated the day at Indianapolis and ate dinner with our worthy Governor Morton, at the Soldiers' Home. How times had changed!

We spent the holiday week just east of Maynardsville, the county seat of Union county, Tennessee. We had nothing to do now but to forage for ourselves and doctor our lame horses that were again troubled with foot-evil. We had plenty of turkeys and chickens here, and a large barn to sleep in at night.

The first of 1864 was a very cold day, and we shall never forget it. I slept that cold New Years' night in the hay-mow of the aforesaid barn. Lieutenant Mitchell, with a squad of the boys, was detailed, on that cold day, to go several miles and to take charge of what was known as Needams' mill. They all got wet in crossing a stream of water and their clothes froze stiff on them before they could reach the mill.

We staid at Maynardsville about 18 days, during which time winter had closed in upon us with all its severities. But, comparatively speaking, we had a comfortable camp with a house and barn to protect us from the storms.

On the 10th of January we had to leave our comfortable quarters and take the weather "rough and tumble." The hills and mountains were now covered with snow. Old king winter had put on his white robe. We did not pitch our tents the first night at all, but hugged closely to our camp-fires, wrapped in our blankets and oil-cloths. On the 11th we marched on to Taswell again where we staid until the 17th, when we started back to Knoxville as guards for Captain Eastmans' train of Quartermaster stores. Now Lieutenant Mitchell and his squad still remained at the Needam mill, and I was sent with orders for them to intersect the company now on its way to Knoxville. We staid over night at the mill, and in the morning we all started, each man carrying on his horse a sack of corn meal. That was a rainy day. We overtook the train at Strawberry plains, near the Holston River. We were up late that night drying our wet clothes, and when we arose next morning we found ourselves covered with snow.

The 18th was a cold, blustery day, and we reached Knoxville about midnight. Here we drew only one-half rations of small stores, and one-fourth rations of bread. but we were well supplied with meal and fresh pork.

The 23d was a beautiful day, warm and pleasant like Spring, and the birds visited our camp in the little cedar grove north of the city. There was brisk skirmishing now at Strawberry plains about twelve miles east of us. A lively time was anticipated at Knoxville about this date. The city was already thronged with troops and still they came. It seemed that our forces were concentrating at this point. The city guard could scarcely keep the streets from being blockaded by the moving masses. On the 25th we moved up to General Wilcox's head-quarters two miles west of the city.

We went foraging on the 26th to get feed for our horses which were nearly starved, not having had grain for three days. The weather still remained beautiful, and indeed, the farmers here began to plow. We left the Ninth Army Corps at Knoxville and marched to Maryville, a distance of 16 miles Southwest. It

was at this place that we joined the old Western Battalion of our Regiment. Our boys found several acquaintances in the Battalion. On the first of February the weather changed and we had a hard rain and a gloomy season until the 4th of the month when the clouds cleared away and the sun once more made his appearance. The boys were nearly all out on picket. It rained again the 6th and was very disagreeable. Lieut. Mitchell, his brother and brother-in-law joined us again after an absence of twenty days. The Lieutenant had been left sick at Maynardsville on our way to Knoxville. The 8th was a clear and beautiful day. We had a heavy detail for picket duty. Feb. 12th, days warm but nights cool and chilly.

Our pickets were driven in from the east side. Our battalion was at once called out to scout in that direction. We reinforced our pickets at several points, saw the Rebel camp-fires and returned to camp about midnight. We were expecting an attack at any hour, but all in the camp were quite cheerful. We were ordered back to Knoxville on the 16th and I started very early in the morning, in advance of the battalion, with a lot of pack mules and lead horses. If there was ever anything I did detest in the army, it was to have charge of a lot of pack-mules. I often wished that I had never been promoted. All the wild mules that could not be worked in the train were sure to be turned over to me to be trained for pack-mules. We always had some amusement as well as a great deal of trouble in educating those wild mules so that they became useful beasts of burden. They were hitched up one behind another and loaded with provisions and camp equipage. They would often get scared and run and kick and wind themselves around trees and then the camp kettles and mess-pans would be seen flying high in the air. When we marched back to Knoxville on this occasion I had fifteen men with me, and we made good time, arriving at the city about 4 p. m., we went into camp on the southside. The battalion encamped about one mile and a half in our rear and we did not see it until next morning. The boys had no supper and this gave them very keen appetites for their breakfast. Winter was again upon

us and we had a few nights of very cold weather with a light snow.

We moved into our new camp just south of the city on the 19th and on the 20th we had a hot engagement with the Rebels out on the Severeville road, east of Knoxville. The battle only lasted a few minutes but was very disastrous as we had six men of the battalion wounded, two of whom belonged to our company. Sergeant Clever, a noble hearted man and a brave soldier, was mortally wounded in this little engagement and afterward died in the hospital at Knoxville. The other man whose name was Miner Richards, stood second to me on the left and was wounded in the leg. I distinctly heard the sound of the bullet when it struck against the bone. The man on my right, whose name was James Adams, also had his horse shot. This was the first real battle that I had ever been in, for as I was Commissary Sergeant I scarcely ever got out of camp except when the whole command was on the march. But on this occasion I had asked permission to go out on the scout, leaving one of the other Sergeants to attend to my duty in the camp.

Captain Herriot also had his horse shot dead under him in this battle, and suffice it to say, the bullets flew thick and fast. General Longstreet had threatened to take Knoxville on the 22d, (Washington's birthday) and we started on a grand scout in the direction of Severeville, taking with us three days rations. We left camp at midnight and marched slowly and cautiously until daylight. We were now supported by a brigade of infantry. At daylight we came upon the enemy's camp which they had abandoned on the previous evening. We now put spurs to our horses and left the infantry far in the rear. We were about fifteen miles east of Knoxville, and the Rebels were on a full retreat far ahead of us. We stopped short, left Knoxville to our right and took a direct route to Maryville, where we re-entered our old camp that we had left on the 16th. We rested here until the 24th, when we started back to Knoxville again. It was dark when we got back to our camp at Knoxville, and thus ended that grand scout of over sixty miles. We had captured one

Rebel, and he called us "Yankee Soldiers." On the 26th we ground sabers. There was much complaint now concerning short rations.

The 28th was Sunday and we had preaching in the camp for the first time in the year of 1864. It rained on the 29th but we drew full rations and therefore did not mind the weather. This was the first time we had drawn full rations in the State of Tennessee.

No wonder that we revived that old song and sung, "Never mind the weather but get over double trouble for Tennessee is a hard road to travel." Certainly no one could ever enjoy a good meal better than a hungry soldier. The spring rains seemed to set in about the first of March, and we had a spell of very gloomy weather. We had to cook and eat in the rain and sleep in damp bunks at night. On the 4th we went on a scout to Maryville again. I was sick that day and having much trouble with my pack mules, I was a little late getting into camp and when I appeared before the august personage of Lieutenant Langsdale, the officer in command, I was not a little surprised to learn that I had been reduced to the ranks for the space of two weeks, for, as he said, the want of proper discretion in the performance of my duty. But, however, after an explanation of the whole matter, this infuriated officer revoked his order, finding, I thought, that he himself had acted hastily and was a little indiscreet. The fact was, he himself was not enjoying the best of health, and he also had been rebuked by one of his superior officers, all of which might help to account for this unpleasant circumstance. We marched back to Knoxville on the 5th, where we were kept busy doing picket duty and scouting.

There was such a demand for pickets now that the Quarter master Sergeant was called out and I had to perform his duty in camp, in addition to my own, by drawing feed for the horses as well as rations for the men. We got marching orders on the 9th to go to the front again. We crossed the Holston river on a pontoon bridge at Strawberry plains, where we camped on the first night. Arrived at Mossey Creek Station on the 10th and

stayed here until the 13th, during which time the main part of the battalion was out scouting, leaving in camp only the sick men and disabled horses.

They got into a fight, and we were ordered up to the front. Two of our wagons broke down in a mud-hole and we were obliged to encamp for the night but reached Morristown early on the morning of the 14th. Here we were again attached to General Wilcox's command. Our battalion was still in advance and still fighting. There was brisk skirmishing on the 15th, but General Wilcox ordered Col. Kline to cease fighting and give his men a little rest. On the 16th it was all quiet at the front, and on this date the news reached us that General Grant had been promoted to Lieutenant-General, and had taken command of the whole Union army. This was a new and important epoch in the history of the war, and great changes were now expected in the army. General Grant in his seige of Vicksburg had gained the confidence of all the soldiers, and they considered him to be the man for those times, and worthy of that exalted position. After eight days scouting and fighting at the front, we marched back to our former camp at Mossey Creek. Had killed five Rebels, wounded eleven, and taken fifteen prisoners. Lieutenant Callahan lost his horse, which broke its leg in jumping a ditch, and Sergeant Adams, of our company, had his leg sprained by his horse falling on it in a charge. On the 21st the battalion went out on a scout in the direction of Bull's Gap, but the enemy was not to be found in that direction and it returned on the 22d. We had a heavy snow storm which lasted all day, covering the ground to the depth of five inches. The sun had crossed the line and this was our equinoxial storm. The 23d was a bright clear day and the sun soon dispersed the snow.

The old citizens told us that they had never seen such a snow storm at that season of the year. One peculiarity of our cavalry was, that the men all rode on their own horses. The horses of our company were inspected about this time, and six of them rejected, and their riders mounted on Government horses.

The ground was again covered with snow on the 25th. A

Rebel Lieutenant who had strayed from his command was captured near Morristown. On the 27th Lieutenant Callahan, of
Company G, with an escort of 25 men under a flag of truce,
took a sealed dispatch into Bull's Gap, to be delivered to General
Longstreet or the commanding officer of the Rebel army at that
place. The flag was halted at the out-post and our boys permitted to go into camp without fear of molestation. The dispatch
was taken to head-quarters and our boys remained until next day
for a reply. During the interval they were visited by many of
the Rebel soldiers who conversed freely with them on the all
absorbing topic of the war. Many of these Rebel soldiers were
dressed in our uniform, while others were poorly clad. They
were getting very tired of the war and many were deserting their
army and coming into our lines.

Some of the Rebels ate dinner with our boys and were highly
gratified to drink some of the "Lincoln Coffee," as they called
it. They said they had not seen any of it for a long time.

After dinner the soldiers of these two opposite armies sat down
to cards, and thus they spent the time very agreeably, while
Lieutenant Callahan took dinner with some Rebel officers of his
own rank at a house near by. Thus the time passed and the
two parties, though enemies, had a very interesting interview.

The answer to the dispatch finally came and our boys bade the
Rebels good-bye, telling them at the same time that they would
expect to meet them soon on the field of battle. On the evening
of the 28th Lieutenant Callahan and his little detachment got
back to camp. Several of the boys of our company had the
honor of being on that detail and when they arrived in camp
they were soon surrounded by all the boys who were eager to
hear the news and all the particulars of this extraordinary event.

On the last day of March we drew our back pay, being a little
over one hundred dollars each. We then received orders to be
ready to march at day-break the next morning. On the first day
of April we marched eastward to Russelville, the train only reach-
ing as far as Morristown. The night was dark and dreary with
frequent showers of rain. We had bought some butter and a

few other luxuries which enabled us to prepare a good supper on
this gloomy occasion. We slept in a barn that night and when
we awoke next morning the command was already marching and
we had no time for breakfast. We ate an early dinner that day
from our haversacks as we marched along. A soldier seldom got
two good meals in succession. The heavy rains had made the
roads very muddy and we did not reach Bulls Gap until 3 p. m.
We went into camp here, the scouts reporting no Rebels to be
found in that vicinity. Here we found Major-General Sherman
and the Twenty-third Army Corps. In this Corps we found the
Sixty-third Indiana and several Ohio and Tennessee Regiments.
Rebel deserters were now coming into our lines at the rate of
about twenty-five per day. They were glad to escape from their
army. One of these "Rebs," who wore a Lieutenant's coat,
said it had cost him $125, in their money, to get thus far.

On the 6th the Rebels sent in a flag of truce with a dispatch
to General Sherman, and of course the private soldiers of the
opposite armies had another interview. At this time the Rebels
asked us what we thought of fighting against England, as though
foreign nations had any sympathy with their rotten Confederacy.

A disloyal element was making trouble in the State of Illinois
about this time, which caused great indignation among the
soldiers in the field, who would have rejoiced to have been trans-
fered from the "Sunny South" and permitted once more to con-
front the copper-heads of the North.

On the 7th we marched up two miles east of the "Gap" on
the Greenville road where we found a nice Cedar Grove which
made us a beautiful camp-ground, the same having been occupied
by the Rebels a few days before. General Manson, with a
scouting party and a flag of truce, conducted a large number of
Rebel families from Knoxville across the lines to their friends.
These families were conveyed in ambulances, and as the train
halted in front of our camp we had an opportunity of seeing that
motley crew. They seemed not to be very happy in the enjoy-
ment of their "Southern Rights." On the 8th it rained again.
The peach trees were now beginning to bloom.

The rain came down in torrents on the 9th and drove us all into our little "dog-tents." Now, when we first entered the field we had plenty of camp equipage, but after we got to the front and had to tear up camp so often and move about from place to place so rapidly, we had to abandon much of our luggage; such as camp-kettles, coffee-pots and mess-pans. But many of the boys had supplied themselves with a quart cup in which to make coffee, and from which they drank the same. Instead of grinding our coffee we used to beat it up with the muzzles of our large army revolvers. Each man now generally carried his own rations, and in his saddle-pouches or haversack could be found at least three little sacks ; one for coffee, one for sugar and one for salt, and we subsisted chiefly on these articles together with "hard tack" and salt bacon.

Our Second Lieutenant, S. J. Mitchell, started home on a furlough on the 10th. The weather was still wet and rainy. Many Union families now came into our lines in exchange for those Rebel families sent across their lines a few days before. On the 12th it was still showery. Rebel citizens were continually being sent across the lines to their friends. Some farmers began to plant corn, but they could do but little farming in those parts that season, for their farms were laid waste. There were scarcely enough rails left to enclose the gardens and make the necessary pig-pens. Timber was also becoming very scarce, for Tennessee had suffered much in consequence of the war. Many Union families were moving up North. We sympathized with those loyal people who had lost almost all they had, and had been harrassed nearly to death by the disloyal citizens and Rebel soldiers. The Rebel soldiers had eaten up all their supplies and now they had to apply to the Union army for subsistance. On the 16th our scouts came in, bringing with them sixteen prisoners, among whom was one James Runnals, who was captain of a band of "Guerrillas" or bush-whackers. Our scouts had killed five and wounded two of this Guerrilla band. Among the killed were four of the Davis family, who had long been known as bush-whackers and traitors of the deepest dye.

The Davis family had killed many Union citizens in those parts, but now their time had come. John Davis was shot down in his own door-yard while in the arms of his two daughters, and his two sons were killed in the orchard near the house. The brother of John Davis who was a Rebel enrolling officer was also shot' and killed a short distance from the same house. This bloody scene took place about twelve miles north of Greenville, Tennessee.

Such had been the terror and consternation caused by this band of Guerrillas, that all defenseless Union citizens had fled to the mountains and neighboring hills to hide themselves from those merciless scoundrels. But so soon as they heard of the coming of the Union forces they came, out of their hiding places and greatly rejoiced with us over our success. Some of our boys who had been in many a battle declared that they had never witnessed so terrible a scene as they beheld on this occasion. And what made it worse, several of our boys who were present and took part in this bloody affair, had been quartered in that very neighborhood a few months before running a mill, and had become acquainted with this same Davis family, none of the men then being at home. To those boys that was indeed a melancholy scene. But owing to the many outrages committed by that family, in that and adjoining counties, we could only conclude that they. had met their just fate.

On the 17th we received a supply of sanitary stores, consisting of potatoes, onions and kraut. For all of which we felt very thankful to our worthy Governor and friends at home. While we were at Bull's Gap, that part of our company which had left us at Cumberland Gap, and had spent the winter in Kentucky, were at Knoxville on their way to join us at the front. On the 20th the beautiful sun once more made his appearance and all nature seemed to rejoice. Fine weather always gave new life and vigor to the soldier, causing him to perform the most ardous duty cheerfully.

On the morning of the 24th, we started on a scout eastward, and expected to be gone six days, but on the 30th we turned up

again at Knoxville, after scouting and fighting about one week. We had a severe engagement with the Rebels at Carter's Station, twenty-two miles east of Greenville, which lasted about fifteen hours. We repulsed them at first, charging across the Wautauga River and taking one prisoner. On this charge we plunged into a mill-race which was very deep, and here several of our boys came near drowning. One of them, (John C. Stevens) swam back across this race holding on to the tail of Lieutenant Langsdale's horse.

The only wonder was that we all got out of that mill-race safely, and none were lost, for three of the boys rolled over and over in the water, and at one time were given up for lost. Never was our company in a more precarious condition; and had the enemy known this, they might have captured the last man of us.

We shall never forget that wet and dangerous affair. Now, our horses began to give out and several of the boys were already dismounted.

This brings us up to the first of May, 1864, when we left Knoxville on our way to Chattanooga. We marched on the first day to Louden, twenty-two miles southwest of Knoxville, on the Holston River. We crossed this river in a ferry boat on the 2d, and on the 3d we passed through Philadelphia, Sweet-Water and Mouse Stations. The weather was now warm and pleasant, and the gardens began to look green with vegetation.

Our route was down a beautiful valley, and the country seemed to be improving in that direction. The groves were now putting forth their leaves, and the green grass covered the fields. On the 4th we saw corn two inches high. That was a very warm day. Passed through Athens, Calhoun and Charlestown. Those towns were supplied with good school-houses, and the people seemed to be better educated here than in East Tennessee.

On the 5th we passed through the handsome little city of Cleveland. And here we overtook the 123d and 124th Indiana Regiments. In these regiments we found some of our old acquaintances (Geo. McCain and Chas. Woodard, of St. Paul, Ind.,) with whom we compared notes and had a jolly time. On

the evening of the 6th, we got within eight miles of Chattanooga, where we encamped near a large spring, and on the 7th we marched into Chattanooga, which was then a great military point. We went into camp four miles south of the city. We were glad to reach our destination after fourteen days hard marching. Our horses were jaded and we ourselves needed rest. Our camp was situated in the Chattanooga Valley, between Lookout Mountain and Missionary Ridge. This was a beautiful valley at that time, all covered with wild flowers, and here too we found wild onions which we used to flavor our hash when we wanted a change of diet. We received many letters from home at this point. The happiest hour of a soldiers' life was when he got a good letter from some dear one at home. We were now reported unfit for duty on account of the jaded condition of our horses. We laid in camp rested and grazed our horses for about one week when a scouting party was ordered from our battalion to go to the right wing of the army at the front to watch for a flank movement of the enemy. Now there had been hard fighting at the front and our forces had taken a great many prisoners and were gradually gaining ground.

On the 14th a comrade (Mr. Tilton) and myself, left our pleasant little camp in the valley early in the morning to ascend Lookout Mountain and spend the day on its summit. This noted mountain is not very wide on top but quite lengthy. There was a good road leading to its summit which is 2,500 feet above the level of the valley below. There was a neatly built village on the top of this mountain called Summertown, where the rich and aristocratic portion of the people of that country spent the sultry season in ease and luxury. We reached the highest pinnacle at 10 a. m., hitched our horses and sat down on a huge stone to rest. From this position we viewed the landscape of the surrounding country and I must say I never beheld a more beautiful scene. It was a perfect picture. How grand and stupendous are the works of nature. Just below us was the green and checkered valley of Chattanooga with its roads leading in all directions, its farm-houses and its beautiful green groves. There

were then many camps of soldiers to be seen in this valley and
they looked to occupy about the space of a common garden.

We went to the main point of the mountain fronting to the
north, and from there we could see the Tennessee River, which
seemed to run immediately under us. The Nashville railroad
coursed its way along the banks of this river. A train of cars
happened to come in while we were here and we could hear the
whistle of the engine and the rattling of the cars long before we
could see the train.

The city of Chattanooga, in the low valley northeast, made a
very insignificant appearance. Above the surrounding valley
could be seen nothing but one continuous roll of mountains so
far as the eye could reach. From this elevation could be seen
parts of five different States, namely, Tennessee, Georgia, Ala-
bama, North Carolina, and South Carolina. After feasting our
eyes for two hours on the magnificent scenery around Lookout
Mountain, we became quite tired and hungry and sought a convalescent camp on the mountain where we enjoyed a good dinner
with some of our "cousins," Uncle Sam's boys.

There were then several large hospitals on this mountain. We
returned to the valley and finally got back to camp about sun-set.
We were a little fatigued but well repaid for our trip. Our
scouting party came in on the 15th late in the evening. They
had crossed Lookout Mountain at a point where hoof-animals
had never before trod. Our horses were again inspected and
several of them disbanded.

The western battalion of the Third Indiana Cavalry had acted
well its part in whatever position it had been placed, and now it
began to grow in favor with many of the field officers, who could
appreciate its services. Company "L" could now also claim
some of the honor due this grand old regiment.

I found in my diary, dated May 18, 1864,

A DESCRIPTION OF CHATTANOOGA.

This much talked of and noted city of that time was but a small
and insignificant town, and any one who had read of it during
those war times would have been surprised to have found so

small a place bearing the name of Chattanooga. It had suffered greatly on account of the war, but the Government had built here several warehouses, depots and hospitals. Excepting these new Government buildings, the town looked old and dilapidated. But it was an important military post, and was then the base of supplies for the Cumberland army.

On the 20th the weather had become extremely warm. The chilly winds had long since passed away, and now we began to dread the sultry days of a summer in that hot climate. And now we began to think that the war was approximating its final close. And why not? Our administration, under Abraham Lincoln, had been a just and impartial one, and everything had been offered for peace that could be offered, and now our grand old Government had grown stronger, and our armies had been wonderfully increased and greatly improved. Therefore we said to ourselves, "*The Southern Confederacy must go down, and it must wither and die on the very spot of its origin.*" Our army was now marching southward, and we knew it was destined to move onward, right on; and we also believed that God would speed us on our way, and that our armies would soon be crowned with success, and that the victory was sure to be ours.

On the 24th we started again to the front. The weather was warm and sultry. Our horses had been recruited, and the men were nearly all in good health and in fine spirits. We passed through Ringgold about noon, and went into camp three miles southeast. A heavy thunder storm came up, and we got a fine shower bath before we could pitch tents.

The bugle called us up early on the morning of the 25th, and we were soon on our way. A dense fog made everything look gloomy. We passed over Tunnel Hill and on to Buzzard Roost. Here we found that the enemy had been strongly fortified, and here they had fought for several days. From all appearance, there had been a large force quartered here. The country around was forsaken, and looked desolate, and we did not at all admire Buzzard Roost, but could have better enjoyed the products of a hen-roost.

The next town was Dalton, which we passed through at noon. This was a beautiful village, decorated with green trees and various flowers, among which was the rose in full bloom. How refreshing was such a spot in the midst of a country so impoverished by armies? We went into camp two miles south of Dalton, where we drew rations for the men, but could only get green rye for our horses. Just before daylight on the 26th our pickets were fired on which caused alarm in camp and brought us out of our tents in haste. At the sound of the bugle ("Boots and saddle") the boys hastened into line. My mule train was a few paces in the rear, and every mule unsaddled and unpacked, but I am sure they were never hitched up in so short a time, for when the command "forward" was given we were all ready to march. We expected a fight here, but soon learned that the shots had been fired by bush-whackers, who when promptly responded to by our pickets, left without further controversy and were seen no more. We reached Resacca, a small railroad station at the crossing of the Oostanaula river. Here the enemy had had another strong position which they only gave up after a long and bloody fight in which both armies sustained heavy losses. The Rebels finally retreated across the river, burning the bridge behind them. In the rebuilding of this bridge it was said that General Sherman had four days work done in forty-eight hours.

On the 28th we arrived at Adairville, Ga., where we were stationed for some time guarding the railroad. Now we received several letters from home, among which was one from the Governor in reference to the recruits of our regiment. Those letters were read with more than usual interest. Late in the evening we heard glorious news from our army at the front, and also from the Eastern army near Richmond, Va. We were all greatly elated and animated with fresh hope. Nearly all the soldiers in the field had the utmost confidence in President Lincoln and General Grant.

June 2d, weather still warm and showery. Good news still continued to come in from the front. General Grant was within eight miles of Richmond, and General Sherman near Marietta,

Ga., and only twenty miles north of Atlanta. Train loads of troops were now passing daily to the front, and General Sherman was rapidly reinforcing his army. On the 7th our division moved up to Kingston on the railroad ten miles south of Adairville. We went into camp two miles west of town where the boys tore down a large frame barn in order to get lumber to make bunks in their tents. Our camp was in a little jack-oak grove near the road where we had very comfortable quarters. But we did not enjoy them long, for on the 9th we moved back to town and camped on the southside. It was a very warm day, and we nearly suffocated while fixing up our new camp. The heat was so intense that even our horses suffered and some of them had the "thumps." ·

I had just got done drawing and issuing seven days rations when the bugle sounded boots and saddles, and we were soon out on a scout. We went about ten miles in a southeastern direction, over a very rough and stony country and through a dense forest of jack-oaks with thick underbrush. We saw plenty of ripe huckleberries but could not stop to get them. It was 10 o'clock at night when we got back to camp. The new moon was now shinning brightly and the glittering stars seemed to be looking down upon us. We really enjoyed the coolness of the evening after a hot days ride. On the 10th we were called out again to scout in the direction of Calhoun where the Rebels had dashed in and burned some railroad cars; but they were gone before we reached the place and we returned to our camp at Adairville, where we remained until the 16th when our company was ordered up to Calhoun to relieve another company and take charge of the place. To guard this railroad and keep the Rebels from cutting off the supplies from our army seemed now to be our main business. We were comfortably quartered here in a large brick depot. Those were the best quarters we had ever found in the land of "Dixie." We were treated hospitably by the remaining citi..ens of Calhoun, and we managed to get a share of their garden products in exchange for our "greenbacks" and coffee. This had been a place of considerable note before

the war, but all the stores and shops were closed now and the vacant buildings only stood as so many monuments of its past prosperity. The court house here had been badly torn up and deeds and other valuable papers were strewed over the floor several inches in depth. The shelving of the stores had been used freely for kindling wood and varnished drawers for feed-boxes. All this proves the destructiveness of war; and life and property do not alone pay the penalty, but society suffers much, and coming generations will feel its effect as they must help to pay the debt. We had a little surprise on the 23d, about 2 a. m. Company "E" of the Ninety-Second Illinois Regiment, came in on the west side of town, where we had no pickets, to relieve us; and as they approached the depot they deployed as if preparing for a charge, and when our outside sentinel saw their maneuvering he at once fired on them, giving to us the alarm. And the next we heard was the command to "fall out" which brought every man to his feet and then to his "port-hole." We had been looking for an attack for several nights, and therefore were easily alarmed. Those port-holes we had made ourselves in the brick walls of the old depot, which made it look like a fort. Now when we found that we had mistaken our friends for the enemy all excitement changed into laughter. It was, indeed, a most ludicious scene. Lieutenant Mitchell wanted to bring his horse in and was flying around like a hen with its head just cut off, while some of the boys stood with their sabers buckled on them and not a stitch of clothes excepting their underwear, looking like so many ghost. Some of the boys returned to their beds, but if I remember right they slept no more that night on account of the loud talk and laughter of the jolly crowd who greatly enjoyed the whole affair. On the 27th a lady came in and reported a squad of Rebels out about four miles in the country west of us. A scout was immediately sent out but as usual they had fled. The firing of our pickets early in the morning of the 28th gave us another scare, and we had another demonstration in the old depot. It was several loose horses this time which came charging into our quiet little village. The vidette on the out-post of

course fired on them, but no harm was done, and our "fort" was again alive with mirth and jollity. On the 29th the weather was still very sultry and the battle was still raging at the front and many a brave soldier had fallen before the breastworks around Marrietta. Trains were frequently passing to the rear with wounded soldiers, while other trains were going to the front with reinforcements. We had suffered much with the heat of June, and now we dreaded the still hotter month of July.

We joined the battalion again at Adairville on the 2d of July. A general move was now on foot and our battalion was to take another position. We were obliged to leave Lieutenant Langsdale, who was sick at Calhoun. He could not endure that hot climate. His health had been failing for some time, and now he was compelled to hand in his resignation and return home. He was a little imprudent at times, but always a brave officer, and it was with reluctance that we gave him up. On the 4th, our National birthday, we were about twelve miles east of Calhoun, in Gordon county, Ga. We thought of home and how our friends were enjoying this great holiday there. As for the Fourth of July, none but loyal citizens can rightly appreciate its importance. We halted on a large plantation where we had a sumptous dinner of young chickens and potatoes dished up in the real old fashioned style. We stayed here over night. Negro women were now busy gathering in the harvest, all the men slaves having been sent further South for safe keeping.

On the 5th we marched on to Cartersville, where we were glad to go into camp after four days marching in the hot sun. Wonderful changes were now taking place in the armies. General Grant had flanked General Lee at Richmond, and General Sherman was marching successfully on Atlanta. We were very busy watching Wheeler and other raiders who were operating in the rear of Sherman's army and trying to cut off his communications. There was an abundant wheat crop in that part of Georgia that season, but very little of it was harvested for want of help, a few old grandfathers and the female portion of the slaves being the noly ones left to take care of the crops.

Cartersville was situated on the Chattanooga and Atlanta railroad, ninety miles from the former and forty-seven from the latter, being just twenty miles north of Marietta. This town, like all other towns in this part of Georgia, was deserted. We had to draw water from very deep wells here and then carry it several hundred yards to our camp. And the weather was so hot that we had to build summer houses over our tents, covering them with bushes and branches of trees. Our commissaries had been replenished and we again drew full rations.

On the 13th our whole brigade was inspected on horseback by Col. Kline, who had now been promoted to a Brigadier. Captain Gattis, of Company "H," had also been promoted to Major and was now in command of our battalion. The 16th was my birthday and I had a good dinner of warm bread, butter and blackberries. Think not that I was then on the decline, for on that birthday I was only twenty-nine. I cared not for getting older if only the weather would get a little colder.

On the 17th our company, together with company "M," left camp at 4 p. m. to go up into the Pine-log mountains in Cherokee county, about forty miles distant, in a northeastern direction. We took with us only one day's rations and had orders to forage for ourselves. We were sent after a lot of leather which had been hid in the mountains, and therefore took with us three mule teams. About sunset while the column was marching slowly along nearly half a mile in advance of the teams, some bushwhackers came out of the thick underbrush and captured six of our best mules and wounded a citizen who was riding in one of the wagons.

The woods were scoured in all directions but not a trace of the scoundrels could be found. A comrade, Mr. Aldrich, and myself had stopped by the way to get some chickens, and at the time of the attack were a little in the rear of the teams, and for a few minutes entirely cut off from our command. We dropped the chickens and rallied to the front, but was not in time to see the "whackers," for they had disappeared through the bushes.

On the 18th we proceeded into the mountains, found the

treasure, and also several head of cattle which we attempted to drive into camp, but the dumb brutes were better acquainted with the mountains than we were, and made so many flank movements that we had to abandon them. We got back to camp late in the evening of the 19th.

The 21st was a day of great excitement at Cartersville on account of the appearance of the Rebels at Kingston the day before. They were said to be 1,500 strong. We got orders to saddle up early in the morning, and we remained in readiness until our scouts came in in the evening. A part of the division stood in line of battle nearly all day, looking for the Rebels, but they had gone in another direction and there was no fighting to be done this time.

On the 22d it was all quiet again in camp, and the 1,500 Rebels turned out to be only a small band of Guerrillas.

Sergeant Tucker, of Company "H," myself, and eight men went out on foraging expedition. We returned to camp in the evening with a good supply of potatoes, apples, and chickens. It was now rumored that we had possession of Atlanta, and the whole camp was alive with mirth and jolity. On the 24th the raiders made their appearance again on the railroad just north of us. A line of battle was soon formed and a scout sent out to meet them and if possible to draw them in, but they had again fled, and our scout returned to camp. The weather had now turned remarkably cool.

General Kilpatrick returned to his command. This was his first appearance at the front after he had been wounded at the battle of Resacca. · A member of our battalion, whose name was Pase, had been captured by the Rebels while out foraging near Adairville, and on this day he returned to his command dressed in Rebel uniform, which he had captured to facilitate his escape from the enemy. He told us of J. V. Offutt, our Battalion Commissary Sergeant, and others, who were captured soon after he was, and whom he left in confinement at Atlanta. He also told us that there were altogether about 2,000 of our soldiers at Atlanta, and that they were so short of rations that

they got only one meal a day. Of the Rebels he said their fears increased as Sherman's army advanced; that they were well fortified, but were despairing of success. Now our company and Company "M" were considered as recruits of our regiment, having joined it long after the other ten companies. And we had been enlisted for the unexpired term of the regiment, but now we plainly saw that we were destined to remain in the army for three years, or until the close of the war. This was the main topic now among our boys, and it caused a little dissatisfaction and much debate.

August 1 the weather remained very hot and sultry. In referring to my diary of this date, I find that I was dwelling on that all absorbing topic,

"THE WAR."

Our nation had been involved in this great war for three long years. And such a war had never been known to exist before in our land. We doubt very much whether any other nation on the face of the globe could have sustained such a large army and have prosecuted such a war for so long a time. But all this enables us more fully to comprehend and appreciate the wonderful power and vitality of our American Government. Our cause was a just one, and while we fought for our rights and for the maintenance of our Government, we were only carrying out the principles of our Revolutionary Fathers, who struggled long and hard to found this same Government. They had made it, and enjoyed it only a few short years, when they handed it down to us to preserve for future generations.

We had great confidence in our modern "Washington," (Abraham Lincoln), who was then occupying the Presidential chair. And we also had equal confidence in General Grant and General Sherman, the two noted Generals who were then at the head of our two great armies. But notwithstanding this confidence and our knowledge of past successes, we could but consider those days as among the most critical and perilous. There was soon to be a Government election, and we were anxious that the loyal citizens might succeed at the ballot-box. We believed

that a victory there at that time would be of more importance than any one that could be achieved on the field of battle.

On the 3d we started again to the front. General Kilpatrick was again in command of our division. He had not yet fully recovered from his wound received at Resacca, but on this occasion he rode in a buggy at the head of his command. Colonel Kline was at the head of our brigade, while Major Gaddis lead our little battalion. We marched about fifteen miles on this day, over a rough, barren country, which had been made desolate by the right-wing of Sherman's army. We saw but one inhabited house during that whole day's march; but many were the fortifications we passed. We were scarcely out of sight of one line of breastworks until we were in sight of another. We were marching in front that day and therefore got into camp a little before night, the rear coming in about 9 o'clock. But on the next day, the 4th, according to the custom for marching, we had to march in the rear of the whole division. One regiment after another passed by us, and then the long wagon train; so it was nearly 10 a. m. before we left camp.

The scenes of this day were much the same as those of the day before, and we marched over many a hard contested battle-field, and saw the graves of hundreds of our fallen soldiers. We advanced twenty miles, and being in the rear, got into camp at 10 p. m. We had now reached the Chattahoochee River, and the Rebels were just on the opposite side. We were only ten miles west of Atlanta, and could now plainly hear the boom of the cannon in that vicinity.

On the 5th, at 1 p. m., we were again in our saddles, and soon after fell back four miles. Our brigade was now sent to the extreme right which was about two miles and near Sweet-water bridge, where we went into camp. We ate the last of our bread and meat for supper and had only green corn for breakfast.

On the 6th, the cannonading was still heard at Atlanta. The bugle sounded boots and saddles at 3 p. m. while the rain was descending in torrents upon us. But we saddled up, struck tents, and was soon on our way toward Atlanta. We approached

within eight miles of Atlanta and went into camp behind a long line of breastworks. It had rained all day and the heavy peals of thunder seemed to keep time with the steady roar of the cannon. We had no supper that night, and with clothes and blankets all wet, we retired to take a soldier's nap.

We remained here until the 9th and were all on some kind of duty. Some were out scouting, some on picket, and others were kept busy as couriers, carrying dispatches from one point of the army to another. So while the battle was raging we were by no means idle.

The cannons kept up a roar both day and night, and on this day the hardest fighting seemed to be on the left wing, and it was thought that the Rebels were trying to make their escape in that direction. Now the battle seemed to be hotter on this day than ever before and we said to ourselves: This is surely the greatest battle of the year, and those who survive it may read of its terrible effects on the pages of history. We expected a glorious victory soon, but we were held in great suspense, for we knew not at what moment we should be called on to take a more dangerous position and a more active part in the great battle.

From the 9th to the 14th of August, we were so busily engaged that I found no time to take notes. But on the 15th, after our brigade had been inspected, the whole division started at 2 a. m. around on the right wing. We took with us pontoon bridges by the use of which we crossed the Chattahoochee river at Sandtown. We reached the river at 10 a. m. and in less than one hour the head of the column was seen ascending an elevation on the opposite side. We expected to find the enemy close at hand and sure enough they were. The train of wagons, the packmules and one regiment of soldiers were left here, but the main part of the command moved forward. In about an hour one of our boys returned, bringing with him a prisoner who had a white bandage tied about his head, which indicated that he had been wounded.

Our battalion was in the front, and they had run into the Rebel pickets about three miles out. The General was yet at

Sandtown, but when he heard this, he and his staff were soon on their way to the front. I was sorry that I could not be with the company on that occasion, but had to remain in the rear with the ever troublesome pack-mules. On the 16th I went with Lieut. Mitchell to General Thomas' headquarters, near the centre of our army, and about one mile in the rear of the skirmish line. The distance from General Kilpatrick's headquarters at Sandtown to General Thomas' headquarters was fourteen miles, and we were establishing a line of couriers between these two points. We climbed upon a huge fortification from which we could plainly see the Rebel fort and their flag, but we were not there long until their sharp-shooters spyed us, and with their long range guns they began to annoy us so that we were glad to take a more retired position.

We spent that night very pleasantly with an old schoolmate whom we found in the 37th Indiana Regiment and returned to Sandtown on the 17th. Our division had just returned from a raid on the West Point railroad. They had cut the railroad and burned the depot and warehouses containing the Rebels' commissary stores. Bushwhackers had fired on them several times but without any serious effect, and they had brought in quite a number of prisoners.

A GRAND RAID IN REAR OF ATLANTA.

On the 18th day of August 1864, Gen. Kilpatrick was permitted to try his skill in carrying out a plan which it was said that Gen. McCook had tried and failed. We started on this grand raid from our camp at Sandtown late in the evening of the above date. The moon shown brightly and it was a most beautiful night. We had only 300 men, and we felt the weight of a heavy responsibility. We knew that we were out on very important business. We had started to make a hazardous march across the Rebel lines in the rear of their army, and we knew that we should soon be in eminent danger. But as usual we tried to look on the bright side, and hoped for the best. But I must confess, that on this occasion, there came over me a feeling of dread, the like of which I never before experienced. It was an awful suspence! We passed

our last pickets three miles out from Sandtown, and one mile further brought us in contact with the Rebel pickets. Our advance guards fired on, and repulsed them, and we continued to advance on them and kept up a skirmish until we reached the town of Fairborne. It was now almost day-light. We had marched and skirmished over twenty miles, and had now reached the place which had been visited and set on fire by our Division on the 17th inst. We rested here about one hour, cut the Rail Road again, and the telegraph wires, and then proceeded across the country to Fayetteville, another distance of fourteen miles. Our Division had been following us up and was now ten miles in our rear. It was to cross above us and cut the Rail Road still further north and between us and Atlanta. Our plans were all laid for us and we were to carry out a certain part of the programme. We captured a train of Rebel forage wagons, two wagon masters, and a number of Confederate Soldiers in the vicinity of Fayetteville. We got several good horses and mules out of the train, and these proved to be the best part of the booty, for some of our horses had already begun to fail. On we went twenty miles further to the Macon Rail Road which we struck at Fayette Station, about forty miles south of Atlanta. Here we cut and tore up the Rail Road, and destroyed the telegraph wires. A train of cars was seen standing on the track about one half mile north of town. When I discovered this I asked permission to go and capture it. The favor was granted, and ten men were at once detailed to accompany me. We charged in upon it without delay, but the train men had nearly all fled into a wood near by. We broke the car doors open with a crowbar and found the whole train loaded with wheat and whiskey. We poured the whiskey on the wheat and set it on fire, (of course some of the boys filled their canteens with this vile stuff) and then Daved Babb (one of the ten) took charge of the engine and run that red-hot and flaming train into Fayette Station. This was all done in the space of a few minutes, and then we started back on the Railroad toward Atlanta, tearing up the track, or rather turning it over, as we went. We expected to meet our Division on the Railroad, but instead of that, we soon met two Brigades of

the Rebels which had been unloaded from a train about a mile up the track in front of us. Now having destroyed about one mile of Railroad track, and done all that had been required of us, and not wishing to contend against such a superior force, we turned off to the left and beat a hasty, though orderly retreat. The Rebels of course followed up and made it very lively for our rear guards. But now we feared a flank movement more than the attact in the rear, and it behooved us to get back across the West Point Railroad as soon as possible to prevent being surrounded and captured. We now thought of McCook and all other like disasters, and for a while we indeed thought that our fate was sealed, and that our time had come, for sure enough the Rebels had succeeded in flanking us at Fayetteville, and at one time we were completely surrounded. There was now no time to be lost, so we drew our sabers and made a desperate charge in front, cutting our way out and escaping from that most perilous situation. We shall never forget the glittering appearance of our sabers at that time as the setting sun shown upon them. They were surely our only salvation on that occasian. We were elate with joy when we got on safe ground once more and realized that we had successfully escaped from so precarious a condition. And now we had only to fear that the Rebels would concentrate their forces and cut us off again at Fairborne. But haply they were not there and we saw them no more that night. We marched until mid-night and had got within six miles of our camp at Sandtown when we halted, dismounted, and every man, excepting the guards, dropped down close by his horse and went to sleep. That was a welcomed opportunity for we had had no sleep for two nights, during which time we had marched over one hundred miles. After having a little brush with a party of Rebel scouts, we marched into camp on the morning of the 20th of August. Thus ended our part of that wonderful raid, to which we can not look back without horror, though we had only lost two men and had one wounded.

THE BATTLE OF JONESBORO AND CAPTURE OF ATLANTA.

On the 26th of August, 1864, after about one week's rest, our whole division left Sandtown at midnight en route for Jonesboro.

We were now to assist in the great flank movement in the rear of Atlanta, that strongly fortified city. We marched slowly across the country, and struck the West Point railroad two miles north of Fairborne. We only had light skirmishing with the Rebel scouts and pickets until we reached the railroad. But here we found a considerable force, and here we had a sharp little fight on the 28th inst. We had often heard the roar of the distant cannon, but now we were near enough to hear the harsh whistle and even to see the great cannon balls as they passed by us, and the bursting shells over our heads. There stood near by an old frame church, which was soon torn down and fortifications made of its ruins. We skirmished with the Rebels during the day time and watched their movements at night. On the 30th inst. we advanced on the enemy and had a hard fight in the evening. We were never so much delighted at the roar of a cannon as on this occasion, when our brass piece opened fire on the Rebel works, for our company had dismounted and was advancing on foot, and the bullets were flying about us thick and fast, and we were just coming into a most exposed and dangerous proximity when our cannon opened on the "gray jackets," and caused them to fall back and give us possession of their works. Our cavalry was now drawn off, and the infantry took our place. The cavalry usually went ahead and brought on the engagement, and then the infantry would come up to do the main execution. But each branch of the service was always glad to have the support of the other.

The last day of August of that year (1864) will ever be remembered by our little battalion of the Third Indiana Cavalry. We were sent to the extreme right, with orders to hold a certain position for two hours. Our boys here built barricades of rails, and waited for the Rebels to advance. They did not wait long, however, until General Clayborne made his appearance with his whole corps of twenty-two regiments, and charged upon their temporary breastworks. Now it was impossible for a small cavalry force to hold the ground against a superior force of infantry. But the boys stood firm and fought bravely until they were

nearly surrounded by the enemy. Then came the terrible disaster of falling back in haste while the Rebels were in hot pursuit. And worse than all, when they had got back to the wood,
where they had left their horses, they were horrified to find that
they, too, had been ordered back, and now they had to make
their way back as best they could. That was indeed a hard
fight and a disastrous battle to us. Our company had two
wounded, one of whom was DeWitt C. Mitchell, who afterward
died of his wound. He was a good-natured, clever fellow, and
we greatly missed him. Now, I was not in that engagement,
but my position during the time of the battle was equally hazardous. I was one of "the hundred men" who had been selected
out of our battalion to make that noted and daring raid on the
Macon railroad, in the rear of Jonesboro, to cut it, and thereby
prevent the Rebels from drawing off their supplies in that direction.

We struck across the country in a southeastern direction, following, as it were, a bee-line. Away we went through woods,
corn fields and swamps, and over hills, fences and ditches. We
charged through the Rebel lines, and on we went in single file,
like so many sheep over a brush fence, until finally we struck
the railroad a few miles south of Jonesboro, and within three
hundred yards of the Rebel pickets. We could plainly see the
enemy's camps. Here, in a few minutes' time, we cut the railroad and tore down the telegraph wires. We had piled up the
cross-ties and started a huge fire on the track, when we heard the
Rebels' bugle sound, "Boots and saddles." We had no time to
lose, and we retreated as we came, excepting that we marched
a little further to the left and west. The Rebels followed up and
kept firing on our rear until we came to a fence overgrown with
vines so that it could not be thrown down. Here our horses
jumped the fence, and many of them fell on their heads on the
opposite side, and here nearly every man lost his hat. Next we
had to cross Mud creek and a terrible big swamp.

We got back to the battalion about dark, much to the surprise
of General Kilpatrick and the whole command. The General

had given us up for lost, and it was with great joy that he welcomed our return and anxiously received our report. We had gained the General's highest applause, and it was said of us that we had won the laurels of that day. We had been fired on at four different times and places, but had only lost one man. In this little detachment Company "L" had eighteen representatives, all of whom returned in safety.

On September 1 we scouted over the late battle field early in the morning, and found that the Rebels had fallen back, and that our troops were again occupying the ground they had lost the day before. We now extended our lines still further to the right, built new barricades, and watched for another flank movement. The Rebels, it seemed, were determined to drive back our right wing. There was heavy skirmishing all along the line during the day, and late in the evening the enemy, having massed their forces against us, came marching boldly up in solid phalanx against our little division. But at this critical moment, to our great relief and their utter surprise, in came the Seventeenth army corps and immediately checked their advance. A heavy battle now took place, the like of which we had never before witnessed. The clash of small arms, volley after volley, was tremendous; and the heavy roar of the artillery caused the ground to tremble under our feet. But the Rebels got the worst of it this time, and we gained more than we had lost the day before. On the 2d inst. we extended our lines still further to the south, and fortified against the enemy. We now had them in very close quarters, and our infantry charged them late in the evening, taking two of their lines. The Rebels were now so completely discouraged that many of them surrendered without firing a gun.

On the 3d inst. the enemy still fell back, and we followed up. And on the 4th inst. our company stood picket at a point where the Rebels could be plainly seen and the whistling of bullets from their sharpshooters distinctly heard. On the 5th inst. we were relieved from picket duty and moved back near the center of our army.

On the 6th inst. we were on our way back to Jonesboro, and

now the whole army was falling back to Atlanta. We were now greatly fatigued and almost worn out, and we marched slowly back to find a quiet place where we could rest and renew our strength. We had been very actively engaged for nearly two weeks, during which time we had actually suffered for want of sleep and sufficient food, green corn having been our chief subsistence. On the 8th inst. we reached the new camp, which had been selected for us five miles west of Atlanta. (Camp Crooks.)

The great campaign was now ended. Atlanta had been taken, and our armies had been crowned with a success, the most brilliant of all during that year; and may I not say that this event was second in importance to none during the whole period of that great war?

On the 10th inst. a foraging party was sent out from General Kilpatrick's headquarters, which came in contact with a superior force of the Rebels near Camelton. A hot skirmish ensued, and the Rebels captured three of our mule teams and thirty-two of our men. Another scout was sent out from our battalion at 9 p. m., which returned on the 11th inst., bringing with them seven of the lifeless bodies of our men, belonging to the Eighth Indiana Cavalry, who had been killed, no doubt, after they had surrendered. This barbarous affair created a feeling of indignation and revenge in the hearts of the soldiers of our division, and especially in the Eighth Indiana Cavalry. Our foraging parties often met those guerrilla bands, and contended with them, but they had seldom found so many together as on this occasion.

On the 15th inst. we visited Atlanta, and viewed for the first time the ruins of that unfortunate city. That surely was the hottest contested battle field in the State of Georgia. There the Rebels had lost many lives and much property. Their manufacturing establishments there had been of great importance to them, and they were such as were nowhere else to be found in all the so-called Confederate States. And, in losing Atlanta, they had lost their great central depot, much of their treasury, and the keys which unlocked the great thoroughfare into their finest lands and most southern cities.

That campaign had indeed lain open the very bowels of that great Southern Confederacy, and its most vital parts had now been exposed to the wrath which was soon to fall upon them. Another campaign, we believed, would finish up the work and end the war. Abraham Lincoln had issued a proclamation to the effect that if the Rebels would lay down their arms within one hundred days, their most southern States would not be invaded, and that their favorite institution of slavery should not be molested. But that proclamation was not heeded, and in about one month after the close of the Atlanta campaign we started across the southern country to the Atlantic ocean. Meanwhile General Hood and the Rebel army had marched around west of us, and were on their way back to Nashville. The last we saw of them was at a little town called Vilaricha, where we charged on their rear guards and captured several of their men. Our company at that time was greatly scattered, being nearly all dismounted and detailed as teamsters and train guards. Byron Dawson, who had been our Orderly Sergeant, but now promoted to Second Lieutenant, was detailed as a staff officer and placed on Colonel Adkins' staff; and I, having been promoted from Commissary to Orderly Sergeant, was now to act as Commissary Sargeant of General Kilpatrick's train; and my duty was to draw rations and disburse the same to about 200 men.

On November 21st we passed through Monticello, a nice little town, though it had been badly torn up by our army which had been passing through it for two days. I stopped at a fine mansion in this town and was invited to dine with some fine looking ladies. I accepted the invitation, of course, as any soldier would. They had roasted a turkey and were expecting some of our soldiers to call on them for dinner. I shall never forget that dinner and the kindness of those ladies. The weather was dark and gloomy and the roads were very heavy. The teamsters were all nearly worn out with fatigue. On the 22d inst. the weather was more pleasant. We arrived at Milledgeville at 4 p. m., and there we met our cavalry which had just returned from the fight at Macon. That was the first time we had seen it since we left

Marietta. We stayed over night there, and in the morning of the 25th inst. the infantry came up and everything seemed to be moving in the same direction, and the enemy following us up. On the 26th inst. we crossed the Buffalo swamps and camped at Saundersville. We started at 3 p. m. on the 27th inst., and marched until 10 p. m. On that day a strange and novel incident occurred. It was a very foggy morning, and even before daylight Gen'l Wheeler had made several charges on Gen'l Kilpatrick, and while the two contending forces were fighting in close proximity, the fog was so dense that they could scarcely discern between the two commands, and the 8th Indiana Cavalry by mistake, formed on the 8th Texas, (Rebel reg't), and while preparing for a charge one of the "Hoosier" boys saw the mistake, and instantly, though quietly, informed the commanding officer, who drew his troops off as quietly as possible, and then poured in a deadly volley upon the Rebel regiment to which he had been so recently attached. And thus that mistake proved to be a success instead of a disaster.

On the 29th inst we marched on to Louisville, and then to our command, which was three miles further east. On the 30th inst. we stayed all day in camp and issued rations. On the 1st of December we started off again in a southeastern direction. Our cavalry had been fighting for five days and the Rebels had got the worst of it.

On the 2d inst. we passed a most beautiful plantation. On the 3d inst. we moved slowly on, with the train of the Twentieth army corps just in advance of us. Scarcely a day passed that we did not have to cross a large swamp, and about dark on that day we came to a most miserable and gloomy one, and the consequence was that we did not get to park our train until midnight. That night was dark and rainy and the roads were almost impassable. The wagons would frequently sink to the axles in the quicksand of the dismal swamp. At a distance in our rear could be heard the steady roar of a cannon, by which we knew that the enemy must be in hot pursuit.

The morning of the 4th inst. was clear and the sun once more

made his appearance to cheer us on our way. We seemed now to have gotten into the low lands of Georgia, where there was nothing but one continuous swamp and bed of sand. On the 5th inst. the weather still continued warm and pleasant. The negro slaves flocked to us daily, and we soon had enough to make a regiment without counting the women and children. They were a motley crowd, with clothes dirty and patched with many colors. Some of the women had young babies with them, and they were a nuisance in the army; but we could not drive them back, as they were seeking their freedom, and so they trudged on after us and we divided our rations with them. The men and boys made themselves useful by helping the teamsters and pioneers.

On the 6th we still marched through the cypress swamps cutting out a blockade and bridging the road as we went. On the 7th inst it rained again, and was a dismal day for us in the swamps, and we only marched three miles in the forenoon, and in order to finish up a day's march we had to trudge along until quite late again. We camped at Springfield, within twenty miles of Savannah.

On the 8th inst. we only marched two miles. We could now hear the distant roar of the cannon at Savannah, and it was thought that the gunboats were engaged.

On the 9th we moved up within seven miles of Savannah. There we stayed until the 11th inst., when we moved around a short distance to the right and close to our division. Rations were again issued. On the 12th we moved again, and on the 13th we went into camp ten miles south of Savannah. That was the day on which Fort McAllister was taken. Great excitement prevailed in our camp, and many were the enthusiastic yells that went up from our hungry boys, for the taking of Fort McAllister unlocked the gate and gave us access to our mighty fleet, and thus opened up to us new and important communications. We had now reached what was called the garden-spot of Georgia—the great rice growing country.

On the 16th inst., at 1 p. m., the first boat from our fleet landed,

and it was welcomed by many yells of joy as it unloaded for us the abundant supplies.

We got through to Savannah before the holidays, and on New Year's day we were quartered within a few hours' ride of that great southern city and seaport. We first went into camp at King's Bridge, about twenty miles west of Savannah, but soon after the holidays we moved up within nine miles of the city, where we remained until the 12th of January, when we moved over to Mr. Barclay's plantation. There we had a most magnificent camp in a delightful grove of live oaks, beautifully decorated with hanging moss.

Mr. Barclay and family had moved into the city, leaving much fine furniture and valuable property in his country mansion, and a few old slaves only remained to give the history of the place. From papers found in the house, we learned that the owner of that magnificent mansion and plantation had been Consul to England.

We found Savannah to be a large and neatly built city, with wide streets, each well shaded with four rows of live oak trees. There was some taste displayed in the architecture of the dwelling houses. They were seldom over two stories in height, but nearly all had a basement, and in entering the main building, one would have to ascend a stairway from off the sidewalk. Beautiful churches were admirably situated in various parts of the city, and these, together with the great stone levee overlooking the river, and the monument of Pulaski in the center of the city, were objects of great attraction. Pulaski had fallen here in the siege of this city in the year 1779. The citizens of Savannah treated us with hospitality, and their general deportment and politeness always attracted our attention.

THE FALL CAMPAIGN OF 1864.

Just before that fall campaign,
Atlanta and Marietta in ashes were lain.
Then onward and southward we trod,
Following Sherman and trusting in God.
Then Milledgeville, the Georgia capital, was taken,
And our cannon was heard down at Macon.

General Hazen at McAllister did then report,
And, notwithstanding torpedoes, he took the fort.
And now when this news reached the rear,
All the boys sent up a loud and hearty cheer.
The Rebels had to go ; for they were surely beat,
And this gave us access to our mighty fleet.
But when we marched into their great southern city,
They said, "Savannah is taken! What a pity!"
That day they and we shall ever remember,
It was on or about the 22d of December.

About the 20th of January, 1865, we received orders to prepare for another expedition; and the main body of General Sherman's army had already begun to make inroads on the soil of South Carolina. On the 25th inst. Lieutenant S. J. Mitchell and quite a number of our company, who had been absent from the command for a long time, joined us. Some of them had been sick in hospitals, while others had been home on furloughs. They were all anxious to know to what command they would now be assigned, as our company was now on detached service.

On the 27th inst. we left our quiet camp, just west of Savannah, and started to march to Sisters' Ferry, about 30 miles north of the city, on the Savannah river. We spent the first night in a most miserable and gloomy swamp. The weather was very cool.

On the 28th inst. we made a fair day's march, and went into camp in good season. Brother "Tom" returned to us from the city of Savannah, bringing with him cod-fish, onions and cigars, all of which were to us luxuries. When in camp at night, our mess was frequently the center of attraction, and we often had visitors who would call and eat warm biscuits and butter with us.

On the 29th inst. we had a frosty morning, as the previous night had been one of the coolest we had experienced in that southern climate, but as the day advanced the weather became more pleasant than usual. At noon we parked our train in a pine grove and waited for a long time on the pioneer corps, which was busy repairing the road in front. The sun had now reached our meridian, and was pouring forth his genial rays, heating up the air and making everything look cheerful and pleasant.

It was quite late when we got into camp that night. The road
wound around through a swamp and over newly made "corduroy." The teams kept coming in all night, and, in fact, some of
them did not get in until the morning. The train had to pass by
the camp of the Second Brigade that night, and some of their
officers had the audacity to claim that they had lost a few boxes
of crackers.

We arrived at Sisters' Ferry on the 31st inst., where we remained until the 4th day of February. This Ferry was about
sixty miles north of Savannah, on the same river. We crossed
this river on a long pontoon bridge, and then for the first time we
stepped upon the "sacred soil" of South Carolina.

It was a fine day, and everything looked cheerful but the ever
gloomy swamps. We marched up the river only three miles,
where we made another halt at what was called the upper landing.
Here we loaded our trains with rations and forage for the expedition. On the 6th inst. we left the Savannah river and started
to cross the Carolinas. The pioneers had just finished
the long corduroy road through the first swamp. We had made
a good day's march, when late in the evening we found that we
had gone at least two miles on the wrong road. The train was
then halted, and a consultation was held between the Quartermaster and other officers, as to whether we should proceed on
that road, and risk our chances of finding another by-road which
would lead us back into the main thoroughfare, or retrace our
steps and go back. The former plan was soon consented to and
the train was ordered forward. That mistake proved to be a very
disastrous one, for the whole train was soon immerged in a miserable black swamp from which we were not able to extricate ourselves until late in the evening of the next day. We had lost at
least one day's march, and our cavalry in the front was still push-
ing forward; the interval between the command and our train
was gradually becoming greater. The 8th inst. was a very fine
day and we made a fair day's march. Bro. "Tom" and I went
out foraging and were very successful. We returned to the train
in the evening with seven chickens, two turkeys, and one pound

of butter. We had also captured about fifty plugs of chewing tobacco.

The 9th inst. was a cool and windy day, and the road was gradually improving as we went north. On the 10th we reached Blackville, a little town on the Charleston and Augusta railroad, and there we joined the train belonging to the Twentieth army corps, which had been marching just in front of us for several days. We now began to approach the front once more, and could plainly hear the cannonading in the direction of Augusta, where Gen'l Kilpatrick was stirring up the enemy.

The 11th inst. was a very pleasant day, and we moved slowly but steadily on. On the 12th inst. we came up with the Twentieth army corps, which was very near the front of our main army, and there we parked our train and stayed until about 4 p. m. of the 13th inst. Then we straightened out and marched four miles when we were again ordered into park. On the 14th we marched slowly. The 15th was a cloudy, dull day, and the smoke arising from the many camp fires made it appear foggy.

A comrade and myself went out foraging and got lost in the woods. But we finally returned to our train late in the evening, bringing with us a straggler from the Rebel army. We were glad to get back safely, for we had been on dangerous ground.

On the 16th inst. we were within sight of Columbia, the state capital; and on the 17th inst. we marched around it, but the train bummers went through, and afterwards marched along our lines, giving to each man a plug of tobacco, and a yard of calico for a handkerchief; and nearly every mule in the train was decorated with ornaments taken from the court house there.

We crossed the Congaree river a few miles above the city on a pontoon bridge. We made a short march on the 18th inst., and on the 19th we reached Broad river. We drew rations and rested there until late in the afternoon of the 20th inst., when we set out to cross the river and push forward.

The weather was pleasant and the country had become more hilly and broken. We had been so long in the pine swamps that

we were now glad to see the hills and get on dry ground once more. We well remember that date, for it was the anniversary of our little engagement at Knoxville, Tenn. We never thought, at the time of that battle, that within one year from that date we should be marching through the apparently God-forsaken country of the Carolinas. But such were the ever-changing scenes of the army. The rebels had refused to accept the terms which might have prevented that last campaign, and have saved their most southern states from that black and blighting streak which marked the course of the Union army. Not a "hen-coop" was now to be left, and that programme was pretty well carried out, especially inside of that dark belt, which was at least twenty miles in width.

We saw many houses enveloped in flames, and the chimneys only were left to mark the places of former habitations. And who could look without pity even upon the wife of a Confederate soldier, who was set out of doors, and stood weeping over the destruction of her home, and surrounded by several helpless children and a few smoky bundles of bed and other clothing? Such were some of the effects of that cruel war.

On the 21st inst. we still continued to march slowly on, the weather being fine and the roads good. My comrade (whom I shall call "Dave,") and I went out foraging again, and found the "Rebs." Having several other boys with us our squad out-numbered theirs, and we drove them back, capturing four fine horses.

Our train marched nearly twenty miles on the 22d inst. Several more of our furloughed boys, who had come up with the Twentieth corps, joined us. On the 23d we crossed the Wateree river, and on the 24th inst. our foragers found twenty of our men who had had their throats cut. They were found at a house ten miles from the main road. This aroused a terrible feeling of indignation and revenge again among our troops, and Gen'l Kilpatrick dispatched at once to Gen'l Sherman the facts in the case, and soon there was a flag of truce sent in to Gen'l Hampton, asking on explanation of that brutal and bloody affair.

The 25th inst. succeeded a rainy night, and it was also a very

gloomy day. On the 26th inst. we marched eight miles, and the roads were very heavy. The wet weather still continued, and more rain fell on the 27th inst., and on the 28th and last day of February it was still raining, and the roads were getting almost impassable. On that day I saw the effects of the inhuman and degrading practice of amalgamation, and modesty would almost prevent one from telling of that very peculiar incident. But having now excited curiosity I must proceed. That strange sight was nothing less than a child whose father was said (by its mother) to be its grandfather. The mother of this ill-begotten child looked somewhat like an Indian, and ignorance, more than shame, was manifested on her countenance. The child had sandy hair and blue eyes, and would have passed for white anywhere. That helped to confirm all the stories that I had ever heard of the amalgamation and debauchery of the South.

From the 1st to the 12th of March I was so sick that I took no notes, nor even notice of the surrounding country, but rode in our little mess wagon, secluded from the outward world. On the 12th inst., however, we reached Fayetteville, N. C., at the head of navigation on the Cape Fear river, and there we rested until late in the evening of the 15th inst. On that date we received a fresh supply of provisions, and that night we spent on the march again. The 16th inst. was another rainy day, and we started late and spent another miserable night in the cypress swamps, marching slowly along over the newly made corduroy roads. Our pioneer corps was kept busy making and repairing the road in front of the train, and lifting the wagons upon it as they came up. We could only march a few rods at a time, and then wait sometimes for hours on the pioneers.

When the morning came and the train was halted to feed the teams, the teamsters were all in a terrible plight, the mud and pine smoke having added much to their already shabby appearance. They were so tired and sleepy that they really felt as though they had lost everything excepting a good appetite for breakfast. Those night marches in such miserable swamps were enough to kill both man and beast. We were glad to see the

break of day, and when the clouds began to disappear and the sun looked down upon us once more, we thought he had never before looked half so brilliant. On the 17th our cavalry had another hard fight, in which the 8th Indiana Cavalry suffered severely. We parked our train early and got a good night's rest. The 18th inst. was a bright, clear day, and we made very good speed in the swamps and got into camp about midnight. On the 19th the weather was pleasant but the roads were very rough. The battle was now raging at the front, and many of the wounded were being sent back to our train. We expected an attack upon our train at any moment. On the morning of the 20th inst. our train and that of the Twentieth army corps were closely parked together, and all the guards were set to work throwing up earthworks around the park. We stayed inside of that hastily constructed fort until late in the evening when we were again ordered forward.

On the 21st inst. it rained again, just enough seemingly to finish up the equinoxial storm. The Rebels were repulsed and driven back, and we again started on, but the train was ordered to be kept as compact as possible.

On the 22d inst. we marched off to the right and struck the Weldon and Wilmington railroad at a station called Mount Olivet, and we were very glad when we learned that to be the place of our destination. We had reached the close of the last campaign, and how appropriate was the name of the place at which we were to end our pilgrimage and to cease from that long and bloody contest. It calls to our remembrance the promises of the sacred Scriptures, wherein it is said that our Savior shall descend on a mountain bearing this same name at that last day when all the former wars are passed and all the people and nations are gathered to the war of the great day of God Almighty and that last and great battle of Armageddon.

On the 8th day of April Sergeant Titsworth and his squad of men, who had been left at the hospital at Chattanooga, arrived. From the 22d of March to the 11th of April we laid at Mount Olivet, and during that time General Sherman's army had got a

little rest, and had cleaned up and drawn new clothing, and the boys all appeared happy again and ready for another march. A few promotions and some other little changes were made, and the clerks in the Quartermaster's department were busy, as was usual after a long campaign. Our train was also overhauled, and a new wagonmaster appointed, who was to be called chief of transportation. New bows and covers were furnished for our wagons, and as we pulled out from Mount Olivet the whole train presented a new and cheerful appearance.

On the 12th inst. the Rebels captured all of our cattle, 150 head, and a strong guard was sent back to protect us in the rear. At 4 p. m., while our train stood in a pine grove by the side of the road, and while some of the boys were eating and others sleeping, the glorious news reached us of the surrender of General Lee to General Grant. That announcement we thought at first to be too good to be true, and as rumors were common in the army, we were very slow to believe it. But when it was confirmed and our boys realized the fact, many struck hands as they talked of home and friends and the prospect of a speedy disbanding of the army.

At Bentonville we found a small Rebel hospital, and the Rebel surgeon in charge told us that he had been left there with fourteen wounded men who had been taken off the battle field on the 23d of March, but that only five of them were then living, and "as soon as they die," said he, "I shall return home."

On the 13th inst. we began to come into a better country, and the roads were improving. On the 14th inst., at 3 p. m., a squad of Rebel cavalry, all dressed in our blue clothing and pretending to be Federal soldiers, came in on a by-road and struck the train of the Twenty-third army corps, which was marching just in front of us. They told some of the teamsters that the Rebels were just in front, and that the orders were to turn the train off on a by-road, and in that way they succeeded in leading off about fifty teams, twenty of which they got entirely away with, having crossed a stream of water and then destroyed the bridge. That

was a real Yankee trick, and they captured in all about one hundred men.

The 15th was a rainy day, and on the 16th inst., at 9 a. m., we marched into Raleigh, the capital of North Carolina. The church bells were ringing, and we soon learned that it was Sunday.

On the 17th inst. we heard of the assassination of President Lincoln, and it almost caused the blood to chill in our veins, for he was not only our President, but he was also our true friend, and the soldiers in the field had learned to love him for his honesty and purity of character.

On the 27th inst. I went to the hospital at Raleigh, and our company was then at Durham's Station, a few miles west of the city, (Raleigh). The 29th of April, 1865, was a day that was held sacred by the citizens and soldiers of the city of Raleigh. It was a day of mourning on account of the death of President Lincoln. All business was stopped, and it was a very quiet day, excepting when the cannon in the court house yard was discharged. Those salutes were fired every thirty minutes during that day, and I remember that there was no sleeping at the hospital on that occasion. At sunset thirty-six rounds were fired, and thus ended that day of mourning, the cause of which we hope will never be repeated on American soil.

OUR COMPANY.

When the war broke out we knew not what to do,
But we joined the army in the year of sixty-two.

In September, eighteen sixty-three,
Away to the field we did flee.

And in Tennessee, almost without rations or tent,
The first cold winter we spent.

We were glad when that time had passed,
For at Cumberland Gap we had had to fast.

We cannot think of the " Gap " without forlorn,
For there we had to live on nothing else but corn.

Clinch mountain we did soon ascend,
And pleasant days at Greenville we did spend.

Finally back to the " Gap " we were sent,
And on to camp Nelson our Captain went.

He was off and gone like a bird,
And afterward we of him but little heard.

Now, I cannot all things remember,
But we left the " Gap " on the first of December.

The weather was so cold that we could feel it pinch,
As we marched on to the river "Clinch."

And here we kept marching to and fro,
And soon Walkers' Ford we learned to know.

All that seems very plain to me,
And I can almost see a six-months chap up a persimmon tree.

Maynardsville I forgot to mention,
As it was a place of no great dimension.

The boys will ever remember the mill of Needam,
That made the flour on which to feed 'em.

In the Spring to Knoxville we went,
And next to Maryville we were sent.

There we joined the battalion of the old Third,
They had never seen us, but of us had often heard.

They all looked hearty and fine,
And the old Colonels name was Kline.

They laughed at us and seemed elate,
When we told them how long we had served in our own State.

And some of those fellows seemed not for us to care,
Until we got into a fight and they found us all there.

Then they ceased to frown on us so,
And said they would give us some kind of a show.

Now in Tennessee we were always at the front,
And if there was fighting to do we always stood the blunt.

Bull's Gap was one of our stations
Near which fell " Davis " and many of his relations.

That he was a bushwhacker was well known,
And he only reaped the effects of the seed he had sown.

We drove the Rebels from their breastworks,
And on to Carter's Station went we like so many " Turks."

Across Wautauga we made a desperate charge,
And drove the enemy with a force not half so large.

Some things here will scarcely bear relation,
But we shall never forget our trip to Carter's Station.

At Knoxville we turned up again one fine day,
It was on or about the first of May.

Now for us there seemed no rest,
And soon we were on our way still further west.

And it was not long until we found,
That, for Chattanooga we were bound.

Sherman's army we joined and were well suited,
And had no fighting to do until our horses were recruited.

In the valley south of town we pitched our tent,
And many a pleasant hour there we spent.

And now to sweeten and shorten the hours,
The Spring had come with all her flowers.

From Lookout Mount we viewed the landscape o'er,
And such a sight we had never seen before.

From Chattanooga and its attractive scenes we parted,
And to the front in the latter part of May we started.

We now marched on to jain the throng,
And soon to Kilpatrick's division we did belong.

The General had been wounded and was quite ill,
So another officer had his place to fill.

In our rear the Rebels turned up soon,
And that caused us to be sent to Calhoun.

There the sultry month of June we spent,
With plenty to eat and a depot for a tent.

Then after making a scout some distance around,
Next at Cartersville we were found.

A SOLDIER'S DIARY.

There our division was again concentrated,
But the General was still absent as we have related.

But from Cartersville we did not move our pegs,
Until Kilpatrick was again upon his legs.

Then to the front we went of course,
For Sherman had sent for our cavalry force.

Then recruited and ready for the fight,
We were at once sent to Sherman's right.

At Fairborne we burnt the Rebels' supplies,
And the smoke of the depot ascended to the skies.

At Bear Creek we burnt the cars and tore up the track,
But being hotly pursued we had to fall back.

For only three hundred men had we,
While after us were two brigades of infantry.

At Fayetteville they tried us to surround,
But our sabers gained for us the contested ground.

The Rebels gave way for they were beat,
And so we continued on our retreat.

All this was done before Atlanta was taken,
But we had cut the road that led to Macon.

When Sherman got ready Atlanta to take,
He sent us to Jonesborough a big noise to make.

We well remember the movement and the fight,
For we started out one very dark night.

We fought by day and slept at night without a "shanty,"
But while we were at Jonesborough Sherman took Atlanta.

For us all this seemed very good,
But it looked quite different to General Hood.

The citizens could not see the point to save their souls,
So they just went back into their little gopher holes.

Now, to give his indignation a little vent,
Next to Nashville Hood was sent.

But the world looked on in surprise,
When Sherman established his new base of supplies.

Across the country and on we went anew,
And into South Carolina went the coats of blue.

The bummers took Columbia but could not "pack her"
So they just stepped in and took a "chaw tobacker."

Now to Fayetteville and on to Raleigh the Rebel goes,
While we halt at Goldsborough to draw new clothes.

Then there was much talk and it seemed not to cease,
It was all about the near approach of a glorious peace.

For Grant had taken Richmond and Lee had to surrender,
Sherman was watching Johnson while his bummers took a bender.

We were often on the line where skirmishers did deploy,
And marched through the South, over Sherman's "Corduroy."

In the hospital we laid day and night,
At peace with all mankind, but the bugs we had to fight.

Three times a day we got our lunch,
And plenty of quinine and milk punch.

They gave us chicken once upon a time,
But it was so seldom it won't come in my rhyme.

But when our State agent from home came,
To look after the sick and to care for the lame,

He gave us luxuries from the sanitary store;
These made us think of home and the days of yore.

For tomatoe soup there was now no lack,
And the sick man soon had a clean shirt on his back.

That agent we gave a hearty greeting,
For he told us at home we would soon have a meeting.

Then we knew that we had but a short time to stay,
And that when we got home it would be a better day.

The Confederacy that had fought so hard to establish its new name,
Had sunk to oblivion and died in shame.

We were very glad to see the end of strife,
For, really, we were tired of military life.

The times were rather hard, though money plenty now,
But Union soldiers would not starve for they knew how to plow.

But when we got home we were all well fed,
And at the first re-union the speaker said:

Oh! ye Patriots, who fought in such a glorious cause,
Ye have saved your country and established its laws!

For you there is honor due and glory pending,
For great was the cause that you have been defending.

On the 12th of May we left the field hospital at Raleigh and went to the general hospital at Newbern. All the sick and wounded soldiers of the hospital were shipped to Newbern on flat cars, without any covering, and the sun was so hot that they nearly perished for want of water. At 10 a. m. on the 13th inst. we arrived at Newbern. That was a beautiful city, with its massive green shade trees, and the general hospital there was all that could be expected of such a place. We fared much better there, and on the whole the place looked inviting to those who had been so long in the field and at the front, where the battle raged and all were exposed to innumerable hardships. In fact, no pains had been spared there to make the sick soldier comfortable. Newbern was one of the oldest towns in the State of North Carolina, and had been once the Capital of the State. It was laid off in good style, and the streets were highly embellished with shade trees, which were so condensed as to give the city the appearance of a vast and beautiful grove of evergreen trees. We left that pleasant little city on the 17th inst., and went to Moorhead City, out on the coast. There we took a hospital ship and sailed for New York City. The weather was good and the sea calm, and our ship being one of the best, we glided magnificently along over the waves. We were then out on the great Atlantic ocean. The ship rocked and groaned all night, but we slept sweetly in our bunks and the morning came at the usual hour. We had then passed Cape Hatteras and were entirely out of sight of land. We cannot describe the magnificent scenes which are common in and upon the great world of waters. Time passed pleasantly until the evening of the 18th inst., when at sundown a cloud ap-

peared in the west, and it was scarcely dark before a dense fog set in, and soon we heard the sailors cry out, "a head wind!" The ship then began to bound and rock as it mounted the huge waves. The sea was agitated and tossed the ship from side to side, and caused it to heave up and down, and if I remember there were several soldiers who were "heaving up" at the same time. In fact it looked for a while as if all on board had the "heaves."

We arrived at New York City at 2 p. m. on the 19th inst., and late in the evening of the same day we boarded a small boat which landed us on David's Island, where we again entered a general hospital.

On the 25th inst. I got a pass to visit the city, and went on board the steamer "Thomas B. Way," which left the island at 1 p. m. and arrived in the city about 4 p. m. The evening soon passed away, and walking on the pavement had made me tired and sore, and I retired at 10 p. m., the usual time for retiring in New York City. I had a pass for twenty-four hours, but took the liberty to double its length, and spent the 26th inst. very pleasantly, riding around in an omnibus, and in the evening I visited Barnum's Museum. I spent the night at the "New England Home," and returned to the island on the 27th inst.

The hospital on David's Island was a nice thing to look at, with every thing neat and in order, but the feeding of the soldiers was done by contractors, and we seldom ever had a more scanty fare. I had suffered much on account of rheumatism during the last campaign, and had spent forty days in the hospital, but finally I was discharged from the service on the 9th day of June, 1865, and was soon on my way home.

And now, as a closing remark, I would say that the aristocratic people of the South had for many years enjoyed all the privileges and blessings of a free government, while they themselves had fostered slavery. So we conclude that the measure of light vouchsafed to any nation is the measure of punishment awarded. And therefore we are not at all surprised that those people did receive a punishment as unique as was the turpitude of their sins.

RANK ❋ AND ❋ FILE.

COMMISSIONED OFFICERS.
Oliver M. Powers, Capt.   Geo. J. Langsdale, 1st Lieut.
Simeon J. Mitchell, 2d Lieut.

NON-COMMISSIONED OFFICERS.
Byron Dawson, 1st Sergt.   Wm. M. Rice, Co. Q. M. Sergt.
General W. McCain, Com. Sergt.   Geo. W. Titsworth, Sergt.
Wm. S. Hubbard, Sergt.   Daniel Lock, Sergt.
Levi Coffman, Sergt.
Jas. S. Thompson, Corporal.   George I. Clever, Corporal.
Bazil Rhodes,   "   Josiah N. Russell,   "
Geo. P. Leatherby,   "   Edward O. Wallace,   "
Jas. W. Haymond,   "   Joel W. Rickett,   "

TEAMSTERS.
Andrew D. Birt and Nathan Peak.

FARRIER AND BLACKSMITH.
Edward P. Mitchell and Perret Newkirk.

SADDLER AND WAGONER.
John W. Sailors and Daniel A. Aldrich.

PRIVATES.
Adams, James A.
Andrews, Marshall E.
Andrus, Washington F.
Bales, Benjamin F.
Bates, John S.
Beech, John.
Blankenship, Charles S.
Babb, David.

Lewis, Cosby H.
Levi, Thomas.
Mathis, Nathan L.
McKee, John F.
McCain, Thomas J.
McCain, William H.
Mitchell, Dewitt C.
Miller, Israel D.

Banta, Edward E.
Brown, John O.
Carney, Stephen.
Colescott, John M.
Cook, William H.
Cole, Martin W.
Cooper, Silas.
Damon, Riley D.
Danbury, William.
Davis, Jeremiah.
Drake, Franklin.
Fouts, Alfred.
Flowers, James.
Griffith, William F.
Grim, Henry.
Hazard, Elias.
Harmon, Nelson S.
Harmon, Charles,
Hare, Charles H.
Heavenridge, Edwin R.
Hosier, George W.
Hollingsworth, Isaac N.
Hubbard, Jacob P.
Hydes, Wesley.
Hoover, Merriman,
Jeffries, James,
Johnson, Lewis.
Johnson, Charles A.
Johnson, William R.
Kirkpatrick, James.
Layton, William W.
Lamb, David.

Moore, John A.
Monfort, Peter S.
Newby, Joseph.
Powelson, John H.
Rochat, James N.
Reed, John E.
Richey, William S.
Richards, Francis F.
Richards, John J.
Richards, Minor.
Robertson, William D.
Robinson, John T.
Sellers, John L.
Smith, William T.
Smith, John P.
Spurling, Tunis.
Stephens, John C.
Stepleton, Zachary T.
Stansifer, Isom.
Stepleton, Wesley L.
Strickler, James P.
Swartz, James.
Tilton, Anthony J.
Utter, Robert.
Wainscott, Nicholas.
Walter, William F.
Wheeler, Charles E.
Winchell, Zimri.
Wrennick, William A.
Wrennick, George T.
Webster, Benjamin F.
Yoke, John T.

RECRUITS.

Adair, Thomas J.
Aldrich, Reuben B.
Ball, Samuel O.
Burgin, Simpson.
Bryant, Zachary T.
Carney, Martin.
McCain, Robert E.
Small, Bud.
Turner, Levi H.

Dalglish, John.
Flanagan, Michael.
Hannon, Charles.
Hamilton, Sam N.
Henry, Thompson.
Hanks, Silvester.
Robertson, Fount.
Stewart, William.
Ward, William J.